I0578773

The Calling

Maxina Storibrook

Silver Grove Publications, LLC

ISBN: 978-1-948869-89-8

The Calling

This author is part of the Silver Grove Publications (SGP) family. If you have any questions or wish to browse our other SGP Authors, please visit our website for books, products, and submission guidelines.

www.maxinastoribrook.com
www.silvergrovepublications.com
information@silvergrovepublications.com

Contents

Chapter 1

Emi blinks blearily at the morning rays, raising her hand to block the brutal light of Soleste. "Are you sure you saw it, Crom?"

"I'm *certain*, Emi," the young man walking in front of her says with a huff. He rakes his dark brown hair out of his haggard eyes. He looks as though he hasn't slept in days. "It's just behind the warehouse."

She exhales in a whoosh. Crom had woken her up just as Soleste crested the wall to the east. She treks through the woods behind her childhood friend, trying to figure out why she decided to follow him. She hasn't seen him since their coming-of-age ceremony over a year ago, and he hasn't made much effort to keep in touch, either.

Fixing the machines in the warehouse is Crom's craft, and Emi works inside Soltara Temple reshelving books and repairing old documents. She can't complain; her red hair sticks out too much when she walks around the city. Staying in Soltara Temple keeps her secluded from the general townsfolk, and she has met several other red-haired people while working there, too.

However, this means she almost never sees Crom anymore. They used to be inseparable when they were younger; they would always play in the woods near his parent's house. On the night before their coming-of-age ceremony, Crom's father had passed away, and Crom had entered the warehouse for his father's cremation. The next day at their ceremony, he didn't talk to her at all.

It wasn't until a month after they began their respective crafts that he finally reached out to her and apologized, acting like nothing had happened. She could tell something was different about him, though, and their friendship fizzled out as they grew busy. Whenever she tried to message him about something, he often didn't respond. Eventually, she had given up on trying to keep in touch with him.

Yesterday night was different. He had called out of the blue with a frantic note in his voice. "Emi, you need to come and see this! It's a *tulip*! From the old books!"

She had a hard time believing him, but his excitement was contagious. She agreed to accompany him out here. After all, ever since the Devastation when Soleste had rained fire onto the world, nearly everything had been destroyed. Entire cultures and species were wiped out. The Elites, an otherworldly species of giants that arrived shortly after the Devastation, had salvaged as much as they could and recultivated life inside their walls, but not everything could be recovered. The tulip was one of them.

The warehouse comes into view. It is an enormous, old, wooden building reinforced with stone that stands four stories tall – tall enough for an average sized Elite to enter it with ease. Most people are allowed into the first section of the warehouse, the forge, but the rest is locked. The duties of the warehouse fall on a few chosen individuals who help take care of the Elites, a tradition that Crom is now a part of. The Elites can enter the locked section with no more than a wave of their hand, and those who work inside the deeper parts of the warehouse do not share what happens there. Emi had tried asking Crom about it once, but he had changed the subject on her.

As they round the corner, she expects to see a random flower that the exhausted young man had mistaken for the extinct flora. However, what she sees makes her spine go rigid and her jaw drop open in shock.

Soft, smooth, red petals curve delicately inward, barely in bloom. A green stem holds the bud defiantly, rejecting everything taught in the records of their world.

"This is unbelievable," Crom mutters, kneeling next to the tulip. His eyes are wide. "I couldn't read the script, but I knew it was a seed. Who would have thought it was *this?*"

Emi's jaw snaps shut at his words. "You planted this? But how?"

He turns to her, and his tired blue eyes watch her for a moment. He points at the warehouse. "An Elite gave them to me a while ago. I think it was thanking me for my hard work."

"What's in there, Crom?" Her voice trembles as she stares at him. Unlike everyone else, she is terrified of what is behind those locked, metal doors.

He slowly shakes his head. "You don't want to know, Emi."

"I do!" Her vision blurs. Her voice rises an octave too high, exposing her fear. "You have been different ever since you went in there! You look at me as if I'm – I'm – "

She cannot say it. No one is allowed to say it. The Elites are their saviors; they rescued the entire planet when it was on the brink of complete destruction. Humans owe them their lives.

But they are terrifying. The smallest stands as tall as a single-story house, and larger ones can reach up to five stories high. Their skin is like polished marble, and their entire frame is streamlined like an abstract interpretation of the human body. Their 'hands' are flexible, malleable rods that taper at the end. Their voices are whispered songs and sound like a choir. When they dance, it rains or snows; when they jump, the ground breaks; when they sing above a whisper, the ley lines of the world are visible.

They are eerie in every way.

Before they are taught otherwise, every child instinctively gives the Elites a look of terror. It seems ingrained in humans to fear them. Many believe it is because the Elites are so large; after all, they can easily kill a person if they step on them or turn around too fast.

Crom is looking at *her* that way.

Crom's eyes drift back to the tulip. "You won't believe it if I tell you. Whatever you do, just don't go to your Calling."

The Calling is a ritual conducted by the Elites a year after someone's coming-of-age ceremony. It is to ensure a person is a proper fit for their career. It is one of three times in someone's life when they can switch careers, so people tend to look forward to it. If someone loves their current career, they aren't cycled out of it, so there is no downside to attending.

"What does this have to do with our Calling?" Emi gestures at the tulip, frustrated. "Quit changing the subject, Crom! I'm fed up with it! What have you seen in there?"

He glances around as though fearful someone might hear them. However, she knows they are the only ones out here. Normally, no one would dare to get this close to the rear of the warehouse; the Elites are extremely territorial about their resting place. If an Elite catches someone who doesn't work in the warehouse so close to their entrance, that person is usually disciplined harshly. It is probably why he planted the tulip here.

His fingers clench in his hair. "Please, Emi, don't go

to the Calling. You might – you might end up in there."

His eyes flick to the wall of the warehouse.

Another chill slides up her spine, and this time, she shakes violently. "What's in there?" she asks again, her voice just as low as his now.

"I can't say."

A feeling of pure dread seeps into her whole body. "We can't avoid our Calling, Crom."

"Act sick. Bedridden. Something."

"Someone will find out."

"You *have* to."

"I'll be dragged to it."

"Then we'll make sure you're nowhere to be found."

She stares at him. The chill is replaced with a pure spike of ice lodging in her chest. She struggles to breathe around it. "We can't avoid our Calling," she whispers like a mantra.

His eyes glisten as he tries to convey the urgency and importance of his request. "You have to, Emi. Your life depends on it."

Chapter 2

Emi stares at the young woman in the mirror. Long, auburn hair frames her green eyes and accents the freckles across her fair skin. She has known she is different, but she never knew it could bring so much dread to a usually festive occasion.

"He's wrong," she whispers to her reflection, and the woman's lips move in sync with her words. "I love my job. They won't take it from me."

When she was chosen to be a librarian and book repairer inside Soltara Temple, she discovered her red hair wasn't just a random anomaly. Most people with red hair are chosen to be the closest to the Elites, thus turning her once-despised hair color into a color of fortune. After all, a career with the Elites guarantees a good life.

She has believed this with all her heart – until last week.

Crom had been adamant that she should not go to the Calling, but she knows better than to ignore such an important ceremony. To ignore it is like spitting in the Elites' faces at everything they have done for the humans. Also, the laws on attending the Calling are strict; if someone does not attend, they will be locked up indefinitely until the Elite decide how to discipline them. Most of the time, it involves banishment across the wall – a death sentence.

When Emi had badgered Crom for more information about it, he finally admitted one small thing behind his vague, yet ominous, warning: only red-haired people are chosen to be taken back into the warehouse during the Calling. It has something to do with the designation they are given during the ceremony.

She straightens her grey shirt and smooths her white pants. They are clothes that symbolize the Elites and are colored the same as their otherworldly forms. Everyone is required to wear this uniform on the days of their ceremonies. It re-forms to the wearer each time, ensuring a proper fit. No one knows the mechanics behind it except that it is part of the Elites' original technology.

Stepping outside her house, Emi takes a deep breath of fresh air. The Elites had danced that morning, and she can still see the faint lines of the world waving through the sky. Light pink flower petals swirl in the air, dancing with the breeze. Everything has been prepared for this festive day.

The very day Crom wants her to avoid at all costs.

Another chill slides down her spine as she steps onto the smooth road leading toward the huge, towering spires of Soltara Temple. It is a massive, elegant structure that burrows deep into the ground, and it strikes awe and wonder into the hearts of anyone who sees it. The entryway itself can be seen from the wall on the outskirts of the Elites' sanctuary where Elite guards stoically protect the enclave.

Never before has she felt this sort of ominous pressure while approaching the sacred tower that holds the knowledge and records of both humanity and the Elites.

She shakes her head, doing her best to dispel the uneasy feeling welling up within her. *He's wrong*, she thinks to herself. *He was just a bit delusional because he hadn't been getting enough sleep. He even admitted he hadn't slept at all the night before.*

She walks calmly toward Soltara Temple. This is a

normal trek for her; when she started working inside the Temple a year ago, she had moved from her parents' house into her own residence in a neighborhood where other librarians and employees of the Temple lived. It is about a ten minute walk, but for the first time since her first day on the job, it feels like the longest walk of her life. Her mind races from one extreme to the next, first believing Crom's words but then dismissing them with ease.

Once Emi arrives at the plaza in front of the Temple, she is so frazzled that she has to pause at the reverse-flowing water fountain to collect herself. She stares at the droplets floating upward, allowing herself to be enamored by the beauty and mystery of the Elites' powers. It calms her, helping her settle down so she can join the others walking through the enormous doors that stretch six stories high.

A mirror image of the plaza rests on the other side of the doors, but this one is inside a massive room. On the far side, a long service desk has lines of people stretching from each of the service windows. A domed ceiling towers above, allowing in golden light through glistening glass.

Two huge Elites stand to the right and left of the desk, observing the Calling with unnatural stillness. Their sculpted heads nearly reach the decorative molding around the base of the domed ceiling, and the places where eyes would be are merely indents on their otherwise smooth faces. Occasionally, they turn their heads toward a different part of the room, proving they are not just statues. They do not make a sound.

Seeing Crom at the end of a line to the far left, Emi approaches him. As soon as he sees her, he hisses, "What are you doing here?"

"It's *my* Calling, too," she murmurs back, smiling at the person in front of Crom who turns to stare at them. "I'm required to be here just as much as you are."

"I thought you were sick, though," Crom whispers, his voice suddenly full of concern. He grabs her arm, turning them away from the curious bystander. He doesn't lower his voice, though. "Are you sure you can walk? What if you have another one of your spells? I'm sure they'll understand if you can't attend; you've barely been able to get out of bed lately."

She stares at him. *He was serious about that*, she thinks. *But I can't just pretend; the Elite would see through it.* "I'm fine; I feel better today."

His hand tightens on her arm. "It's not too late. I don't want you to pass out or for anything *else* to happen."

His emphasis on the word 'else' makes the hairs along her neck stand up. She forces a smile onto her face. "That's why you're here, right? To help me out if anything *does* happen?"

His hand drops as he gives her a rueful smile. "I should've known." He shoves his hands into his pockets. "I'll do my best, but I can't promise great results!" He winks, hiding the ominous message behind his words.

They wait for their turn. One person after another steps up to the counter, holds a plain-looking, slate grey stone in their hands, and then reveals it to the clerk to show the image newly engraved on it. Based on what it is, they either receive a letter stating they are staying on their current career path or instructions telling them to step into the next room to discover their new career.

The closer they approach the desks, the longer it seems to take. For a moment, Emi wonders if an Elite is slowing down time, but that doesn't make sense. Why would they do that? There is no point. Emi cannot escape even if she wanted to.

Finally, it is Crom's turn. He steps up and holds out his hand, taking the offered stone from the clerk. He covers it with his other hand, waits a few seconds, and then uncovers it to reveal the image now etched into the solid stone. A simplistic silhouette of a house is ingrained into it.

The clerk reviews Crom's documents from a platform on his right, flipping through it a bit before murmuring, "You have Alette's Hearth. This aligns with your current career; take this." He hands Crom a letter, but both of them know what it says; he is keeping his current job at the warehouse.

It is now Emi's turn.

She steals a quick breath before stepping up to the clerk's window. He holds out his hand wordlessly, poised to drop the smooth stone. She stares at it for a moment before dispelling her doubts and holding out her hand.

Crom is wrong, she tells herself yet again. *He is* wrong. *Nothing bad will happen, and this will show him.*

She has been studying the different sigils diligently in her spare time; certain ones correspond to certain jobs, and others might signify a change. It is a mystery on why Elites chose these specific designs, but she knows the names are just for reference. Elites don't name things; only humans do.

Emi expects to get one of three different types of sigils: a cathedral, a house, or a fire. These signify that she will either stay as a book repairer or progress to a higher position, but she will remain in the library regardless of the outcome of her Calling.

The cool stone falls onto her palm, and she covers it. She wishes fervently that the symbol will be the cathedral; if she gets that, her studies will veer toward the ancient tomes and books that are sequestered on the lower floors, maintained only by a select few individuals. Ever since she learned about them from her lead librarian, Sophie, she has been interested in the older records.

The stone warms in her palm. She uncovers it, looking down in both fear and eagerness.

The Witch's Doll looks up at her.

Chapter 3

Emi stares at the silhouette of a woman cradling a baby. It is called the 'Witch's Doll' because the woman is hunched over and holds the bundle away from her as though looking at it instead of cradling it. It is a rare sigil; it's only ever seen once every two to three Callings. The Elites consider people who receive this sigil special, but there is one consistent thing that always follows receiving the Witch's Doll.

The person disappears.

Emi cannot move. The clerk reaches forward and hands her a letter, telling her to step into the other room. She just stands there, though; the only thoughts running through her mind are Crom's words warning her not to come today and the fact that all other recipients of this stone have disappeared off the face of the world.

As she stares at it longer and longer, it looks less like an old woman holding a babe and more like an Elite holding a human. She shivers violently.

Crom grabs her arm, pulling her away from the counter while hissing in her ear. It takes her a moment to register his words.

"You need to collapse now. Pass out – or do your best to. If I can manage to claim you have some type of medical problem, we can still get you out of here, but it has to be *now*, Emi."

Emi's knees buckle from underneath her. She can't walk any farther – not because she doesn't want to, but because her body is no longer responding to what she tells it to do. Before she can respond to Crom, the world blacks out, and she knows nothing but the darkness of her own mind.

———◆———

The first thing Emi sees is pretty, amber light shining through the stained glass in the vaulted ceiling high above her. She stares at it for a moment, trying to remember why she is in the Temple.

A familiar face blocks out the view, and long, golden hair tickles her cheeks.

"Emi, what happened?" Patri asks softly, tucking her golden locks behind her ear. "Crom said you collapsed."

"Where am I?" Emi asks, though she has a suspicion.

"In the waiting room." Patri glances around. "Crom was here, too, but since he didn't have to change jobs, he was escorted out."

Emi struggles to sit up. Patri helps, steadying her and rubbing her arm comfortingly. "How did I get here?"

"An Elite brought you in." Patri looks a little unhappy. "Crom said you need to go to the medical facilities, but the Elite refused. As soon as I saw it was you, I ran over and said I can help."

Emi gives her friend a wobbly smile. "Thank you. So... you're switching, too?"

Patri nods, holding up her stone. The symbol on it is a bulging, curved triangle with spindles connecting the three sides. It is called the Healer's Wheel. Patri had been part of the library team with Emi, but everyone knew she would have been better suited as a doctor or nurse. It looks like she will get her wish.

"I'm so happy for you," Emi congratulates, though her words sound hollow.

Patri gives her a strange look. "What did you get? I thought for sure you would be staying in the library."

Emi looks down at her hand. Despite passing out, her fingers are still clenched tightly around the stone. She slowly opens her fingers and exposes it.

Patri gasps in sympathy. She fights to smile. "The… the Elites must be happy. They have a new assistant now."

Emi looks down at the Witch's Doll as her heart twists in her chest. She had forgotten that part of the position; the Elite claim that whoever gets this stone becomes an integral part of the Elite to keep peace and order to the shattered, barren world. Humans, of course, interpret their abstract explanation as best they can, thinking that the people who are chosen work alongside the Elite.

Crom's face pops up in Emi's mind, and she shivers violently. She rubs her arms almost like an afterthought. "Yeah."

Before Patri can say anything else, a small Elite enters the room from a side door. It walks up to them and wordlessly holds out one of its spindly 'arms' to Emi.

She hands over her letter and the stone. The single-pointed arm splits apart into smaller tendrils that open the letter and hold it up like a multitude of fingers. It beckons her to follow it.

Having no other options, she does.

Last year, when Emi and others the same age as her had had their coming-of-age ceremony, they went into rooms very similar to the one she enters now. It has a large chair for an Elite and a regular chair for the human; floating, curved, glass monitors covered in strange symbols and designs surround the Elite. On the other side of the room, another door leads to a hall that exits outside.

The Elite guiding Emi does not stop at the chairs. It walks past the other Elite and opens the door, turning to her expectantly. She pauses and glances at the chairs and the sitting Elite, confused that she is not getting an explanation of her new duties.

The Elite walks back over and stands in front of her. Looking up at it, she is a bit surprised how *small* this one is in comparison to the others. Smaller Elites aren't uncommon, but they are not seen as much because they can't communicate as well as the larger ones. This one is probably the smallest one she has ever seen. It is only about twelve feet high.

It bends down, bringing its face to the same level as hers. The abstract curvatures suggesting facial features move subtly, and she swears that if the Elite could feel and express emotion, it would be smiling right now. It holds out its arm, and it breaks apart again to form smaller tendrils that gently wrap around her hand. It is cool and smooth like marble, and a soft zing of a strange current zips through her fingers. She shivers again.

It silently guides her out the door and down a deserted path. Most people in front of the Temple are telling their friends and family how their Calling went. The Elite leads Emi away from the crowd, navigating through winding streets and approaching the tree line at the edge of the city.

As soon as she realizes where they are heading, she tries to yank her hand free. It doesn't budge from the giant's grip, but the Elite pauses and turns its head toward her.

"Where are we going?" she demands, her voice shaking.

It reaches up with its other arm and pats her on the head. It is a simple, awkward motion, but it somehow feels… familiar. She is reminded briefly of her recently-departed mother who had passed away in the hospital.

The Elite sticks out like a marbled needle against nature's backdrop as it takes her to the warehouse.

Chapter 4

The warehouse quickly comes into view. The Elite guides Emi through the first section, and they pass by workbenches, crafting tools, half-finished projects, hot forges, and soldering stations. It pauses at a pair of large metal doors on the other side, and it whispers out a strange, garbled song. Emi stares at it for a moment, wondering just how young this Elite is; it can't even use its native language that well.

They step into a brightly-lit room. She shields her eyes, letting them adjust as the doors shut behind them. As soon as she can see, she chokes back a scream.

Emi now knows why Crom doesn't want her here.

Several small Elites lie on the floor at an angle, their insides hollow. Humans are being inserted into several of them, looking sedated as the smooth marble inches over their skin and covers them completely.

At the other side of the room, a fairly large Elite is propped against the wall, barely moving as other Elites make precise cuts at its torso. They pull out a strange, dry husk and toss it to the side. They then lift something – no, *someone* – and place the person inside the opening in the Elite.

Along the right side of the room, many humans are being treated by Elites as though they are getting check-ups at the hospital. They check the humans' vitals via removable cuffs on their wrists, look at their throats, take blood samples, and give them cups of food. Almost everyone seems a little loopy as if they had been drugged.

There are a few humans walking around in pristine, marble-patterned coats, but they look as though they have completely shut off their emotions.

Emi covers her mouth with her free hand, barely able to keep from screaming. Bile rises in her throat, and she is suddenly tempted to give them all a sample of what is in her stomach. Now, she knows why Crom had avoided her shortly after he had started working here. After all, there is one feature that is shared between most of the humans in this room.

They have red hair.

———◆———

Crom's legs don't move fast enough across the road. Even though the huge clock tower is far behind him, he can still hear the second hand counting down. The incessant *tick, tick, tick* burns into his mind, forcing him to realize that his plan didn't work.

They have Emi.

He staggers into the woods, making a beeline through the trees and shrubbery. He doesn't need the pathways or paved roads; he knows how to get to the warehouse by heart. Those routes take nearly twice as long, anyway. Emi doesn't have that kind of time.

I have to make it. I have to save her.

He has already seen what happens to those who enter the Elite's hollow innards. They are tied to a metal frame and lowered into the Elite where a silvery liquid encapsulates them. When they are pulled out, they are physically drained as though their very life had been sapped away. Their skin appears red as though they are covered in burns, and they are either half-crazed or in a dreamy stupor. The caretakers, humans who had once gone through the procedure themselves, call this procedure an 'energizing session.'

Crom cannot bear to witness Emi suffer the same horrid fate as the others. The Elites may believe that energizing with them is an honor, but he knows better. Humans are nothing more than fodder to them, thrown away once they run out of life.

His foot catches on a root. He nearly sprawls head-first into a thorny bush, but he manages to catch himself on a nearby tree. Straightening, he takes a ragged breath before resuming his sprint through the trees, dodging branches and roots in his way.

He makes it to the warehouse in record time. Slipping in through a side door, he sprints to the small entrance meant for humans. He wishes that Emi is different; that she had stayed in the library.

If a redhead is selected, they are always energized first to determine their fate. He has yet to see anything different.

He slaps his keycard against the access panel on the side of the warehouse farthest away from the city. It opens with a soft *beep* that echoes in his ears.

Slipping in, he fervently glances at the Elites that are stretched out throughout the room. They are completely still like the statues they emulate. He spots a red-haired man being escorted by two dazed-looking humans, but not a woman.

Crom exhales slowly. He still has time. Working his way to the cots, he creeps along in the shadows until he finds her.

Emi sits on the edge of one of the hovering tables and stares at the cuff around her wrist that reads her vitals. The monitor on the side of the table blips softly, giving away her abnormally high heart rate.

She's in shock, he realizes. *I can't blame her; it's been nearly a year, and I'm still trying to come to terms with this place. Not that I ever will.*

They had been taught since a young age that the Elites protect them, not use them like fuel and then toss them aside.

As he walks toward her he realizes he will have to put his plan into motion tonight.

"Emi?" he calls out to her gently. She doesn't respond. "Emi, it's me, Crom."

She continues to stare at the cuff without blinking. He reaches out and touches her wrist, and she jumps. The look in her eyes has him pulling her into a hug.

"C-Crom…" she chokes out, squeezing his hand tightly while gripping his shirt with her other hand. "I… I…"

"It's all right," Crom breathes, running his fingers through her silky, red hair to try to help her calm down. He has always found her hair absolutely stunning, but right now, all he can see is how much of a curse it is. "I'm here."

"Wh-what do I do?" Her hand grips his shirt tightly, so he can't pull back to see her face. He glances around nervously, worried that someone might notice and grow suspicious. "I'm so scared."

"I'll protect you." He squeezes her to himself, bringing his face closer to her ear. "But right now, I need you to let me go and tell me what they've done so far."

She slowly releases his shirt, allowing him to pull back. He kneels in front of her as she swallows hard and touches the side of her neck. "They… they put a device here and pressed a button. It felt like something was pulled out."

"A microchip," Crom says softly, and at her confused look, he continues. "It was put in you at birth so the Elite can find you wherever you go. For some reason, they have to take it out when you're about to be energized."

"E-energized?"

Crom glances toward the opened Elites where the red-haired man is being lowered into the gaping hole in one of them. He feels her shiver and takes her other hand. She squeezes his fingers tightly.

"They use us as a source of energy," he explains as gently as he can. "They keep us alive as long as possible, but in the end, well… I think the longest one survived for about thirty years."

She stares at him, her face contorting into pure terror. She sucks in a breath, and he quickly clamps his hand over her mouth before she can emit a sound. Hot tears strike the side of his hand.

"We still have time," he whispers, "but I need you to do *exactly* as I say, you hear?"

She nods as he removes his hand. He sits next to her, and the cot's hovering mechanics readjust to the added weight. She leans against him, and he glimpses his fingers turning a reddish-purple from her death grip.

"Keep looking shocked, no matter how drugged you feel. They won't put you into an Elite if they think you're emotionally unstable. You're young, too, so they will probably want to put you in one of the older ones. None of them are scheduled to come in today, though, so we'll leave tonight."

She looks at him. "Where will we go?"

He stares into her pretty green eyes.

"Outside the wall."

Chapter 5

Emi stares at Crom. He can't actually mean it; there is nothing beyond the protective wall but a barren wasteland full of wild, mutated animals that will eat a human in a heartbeat. Someone is more likely to die of poisoning, dehydration, or being eaten alive than actually make it to another settlement. Everyone knows this. Even the people who are allowed to visit the wall say the same thing: it is uninhabitable. Strange creatures howl throughout the day and night; deformed animals claw at the base of the wall, and misshapen stone giants wander the twisted forest.

Beyond the wall is a death sentence.

"We can't," Emi whispers, trembling. "There's no way."

There's no way to get out. There's no way to survive.

"We can. I've found a way."

"But… the Elites protect us," she says monotonously, repeating the mantra. She cannot wrap her mind around what is going on; everything seems unreal as though she is dreaming. "They help us grow into our best potential. If it wasn't for them, we would have been wiped out long ago."

"That's what they want us to think." Crom takes a quick breath before continuing. "I know it's dangerous, but it's better than seeing you waste away inside an Elite. I've seen what happens when someone is pulled out of them; most are half-insane, always blubbering nonsense. Some are just barely hanging on. They all look drained; their sanity, their health… They're never the same again."

His eyes glisten. "I couldn't stand it if that was you."

She stares into his eyes. Emi knows it is bad to go against the Elites' decision on anything. Depending on the offense, a person can even be banished beyond the wall, which is the equivalence of being put to death. However, Crom is saying that her current fate is worse than being eaten alive by the monsters beyond the wall.

That alone makes her sick.

Emi clenches his hand even tighter. "I trust you," she breathes, closing her eyes as her head dips forward. She feels his forehead against hers, and his warm breath tickles her chin. She welcomes his comfort; it is the one thing that is keeping her from completely losing her sanity.

"Is there anything you want from your house before we leave?" he asks, not moving.

"No." She opens her eyes and stares at their linked hands on top of her white uniform. "Actually, a change of clothes would be nice."

"I can do that." He pulls away, but she doesn't release his hands. He tugs on them gently. "Emi, I need to prepare for tonight."

Her breath catches in her throat. Her heart thumps heavily and rapidly, hurting with every pound against her ribcage. "Are you sure I won't be taken away today?" she breathes, her vision blurring again.

He squeezes her hands reassuringly and rests his forehead back on top of hers. "You definitely won't. Just keep acting shocked. I'll get you out of here, Emi. I promise."

A tear slides down her cheek. "Don't leave," she barely breathes. She chokes back a sob. "Don't leave me here."

"I'll be back." He presses a swift yet firm kiss into her hair, leaving quickly.

Emi stares at her hands as tears slide down her cheeks,

leaving icy trails in their wake. She feels so cold. Her fingers and toes look bluish-purple in the sterile light.

Someone stops in front of her. Jerking her head up, she swallows Crom's name. A young, red-haired woman watches her, her soft blue eyes expressionless.

"My name is Sinora. I will be your caretaker for the time being." She holds out her left hand. "Arm, please."

Emi lets Sinora check her vitals through the cuff on her wrist. Emi's pounding heart rate and spiked blood pressure blip across the screen, the numbers flashing red. A little red symbol lights up in the bottom right corner.

"You need to settle down," Sinora admonishes, pushing on Emi's shoulder until she is lying down. "You have an honorary position, Queremi. You do not need to be afraid. You're going to be energized with the most esteemed Elite; you will share in their knowledge and ways, becoming more than just a human."

"More than… human?" Emi repeats. Hearing her full first name is strange; most people know she doesn't go by it. Seeing a flash of light out of the corner of her eye, she turns her head to see the woman preparing a syringe with blueish-purple fluid in it. "What is that?"

"A calming solution," Sinora replies, giving Emi a smile that doesn't reach her eyes. "A very prominent Elite picked you, and it is coming in today. We need you to be calm for the initial contact."

"B-but I just got here," Emi argues weakly. "I-I can't."

Sinora shakes her head. "That doesn't matter. You should be honored; this is the oldest Elite, one with the most knowledge about everything." She gives her another fake smile. "You will learn so much."

Emi's breathing becomes shallow and rapid. "No." The caretaker taps her arm, searching for a vein. She yanks away, but Sinora clamps her hand around Emi's arm and holds it still. "No!"

Emi feels the prick of the needle. It slides into her skin, invasive and cold. She can feel the liquid moving through her veins and slowing her movements. Her head lolls to the side as her eyelids grow heavy.

She stares across the room, fighting to stay awake. The last thing she hears before fully losing consciousness is Sinora's cold, monotonous voice.

"It will wear off in an hour, though you will sleep until the Elite gets here. You will then have the honor of enlightenment, and you will understand everything. You are fortunate, Queremi; if you accept the Elite Elder, you will not be like the others – you will be like me. Still sane."

Chapter 6

Crom tries not to think too hard about what he is doing as he grabs some undergarments from a drawer and shoves them into a bag before moving to the next set of clothes.

I hope this will be enough, he thinks after tucking a couple shirts into the bag. He doesn't want to take too much in case they send someone for more; it can't look like he is about to escape with her. This way, if anyone asks, he can say he had some down time and picked up a few clothes for her.

He glances around, feeling awkward to be in Emi's bedroom. The back door had been unlocked when he had arrived, so he did not have much trouble getting inside. The private residence is sparsely furnished, reflecting the lifestyle of most librarians. A few documents rest on her desk, and her bed is neatly made. A floor-length mir-ror next to her closet door is the most ornate out of every-thing there.

Crom walks up to it, staring at himself in the reflec-tion. The young man who stares back looks rugged yet skittish, ready to fight or flee at the slightest provocation. He rubs his five o'clock shadow, now self-conscious of his appearance.

Mirrors are rare nowadays; the Elite don't like them, so they ban their presence wherever they are. However, they do not mind if they are in people's homes. He has heard rumors that the sight of themselves causes them to freeze up, but he doesn't dare try it for fear of what they might do to him.

Emi had told him once that she had been given her mirror as a family heirloom shortly after she had moved into her new residence. She had messaged him about it, but he could barely look at his communicator back then. He had been physically sick for several days when he had first started working. After he had finally grown... *accustomed* to the work, he would go home and curl up into a ball in his room and try not to think about anything he had done that day. Emi's messages had always distracted him, but he didn't dare reach out to her; he was terrified of telling her about his job and had no clue what he would have said.

Clenching the bag's strap tightly, Crom turns to Emi's bedside table and yanks open the drawer. He doesn't have time to think about any of that; the longer he is away from the facility, the sooner they will suspect he is up to something. Many of the others have been brainwashed; their heads are full of drugs and promises. It had taken him a couple weeks before he had managed to convince them that he was one of the 'cooperative' ones and didn't need to be drugged.

He can never understand the people who have been energized and retain some semblance of sanity; they had been *inside* an Elite. They experienced whatever that was like; 'enlightenment,' they call it. They always say he will never understand and just smile that creepy smile that reminds him of the Elite.

His hand trembles as he pulls out a book from Emi's nightstand. Momentarily distracted from his own thoughts, he stares at it dully. It doesn't have a title or description on it anywhere. It takes him a moment to realize this must be a journal – one of those rare blank books people used to write their thoughts in.

Nowadays, these original journals are extremely rare to find; the librarians can make something similar, but they are never perfectly bound like this one. Crom opens it and traces the straight lines where one would write. The curving letters on the page catch his eye, and he follows them before realizing what he is doing.

> ~   *Aug 11, 2147*
>
> *I tried reaching out to Crom again earlier today. I know he received my message, but he didn't respond. He never responds anymore. Did I do something to anger him? Is he mad at me? We had always been close before, so I just don't understand. I know he doesn't want to work at the warehouse like his father, but it isn't like I had anything to do with the selection.*
>
> *I'm happy to be a librarian, though. It's what I always wanted! I just want to share my excitement and all the things I've learned. I know he has always been interested in the outside world before the Devastation, and I learned some neat things about the original culture of our area today.*
>
> *Instead, he is shunning me. I feel so unwelcome now. Maybe I should stop trying.*

His fingers trail across the bottom of the page where the ink blurs and the paper warps. He has heard of this material doing this if it gets wet.

A flash of guilt stabs through his chest. He knows he doesn't always respond to her lighthearted messages about her day and the random facts she learns, but he didn't think it would have hurt her so much.

He turns a couple pages, unable to stop from reading another entry.

~   Sept 27, 2147

Sophie brought in her little baby today! She was so cute with those bright blue eyes and blonde hair. I couldn't help but coo over her with the others. She was so cute! I actually learned today that blue eyes are a mutation! Who would have known?!

I love repairing these old books. I get to learn so many interesting things!

I thought about messaging Crom about it, but I don't think I will. I don't want to get my hopes up that he might actually respond for once — not that he will. We used to be such good friends. Even though I've made new ones, I just wish we hadn't grown so far apart. I miss him.

Look at me, rambling about Crom when I told myself I'd stop. I need to get over him. This happens, right? Even Sophie said so. A lot of friendships die off after people receive their duties. She had a childhood friend who stopped speaking to her after their coming-of-age ceremony, too. I just didn't expect it to happen to us.

But enough of that! Tomorrow, I'm going with Sophie and Patri into town to go shopping. I finally have enough money to get a few new outfits. I'm so excited!

He closes the book, feeling as though the room is collapsing around him. "I'm the worst," he whispers, his vision blurring. He angrily swipes at his eyes with his sleeve.

I'll just have to make it up to her somehow, he thinks resolutely.

Just as he drops the journal into the bag, his transponder goes off in his pocket. Tugging it out, he fumbles with the buttons and squints at the screen to read the tiny script.

"Shit," he curses, shoving it back into his pocket and scrambling for the door. He sprints down the road, already knowing he won't make it in time.

The Elite Elder is getting an unscheduled transfer in fifteen minutes, and the energizer is Queremi Dyram.

Chapter 7

Emi can hear people talking around her, but she is unable to bring herself to focus on their words. Her eyelids feel glued shut, and it is too much effort to open her lips. She wants to go back to sleep, but she has a nagging feeling she is forgetting something important. There is a reason why she should stay awake; she shouldn't be resting. She needs to… to…

What does she need to do?

She finally musters the strength to open her eyes. Blinking groggily, she realizes she is upright and propped against a strange frame-like device. She turns to the right where a man is strapping her arm to the frame.

He smiles at her. He has a strange, vacant look in his eyes, and Emi frowns. "I see the drugs are wearing off, Miss Queremi. Just in time, too; your host is ready."

She tries to respond, but a thin, sticky cloth covers her mouth and keeps it shut. She jerks in surprise, but her arms and waist are restrained by thick bands cinching her to the frame. She can't move.

She tries demanding to know what he is doing to her, but only a garbled sound comes out. She yanks even harder against her bonds, snapping out of her groggy state as adrenaline courses through her veins.

"Please calm down, Miss Queremi," the man encourages, sounding as though he is in a daze. "This will go much easier if you do."

She tries shaking her head to free herself of the cloth. Where is Crom? He had said he wouldn't let this happen. What happened to him? How long has she been asleep?

She is jerked into the air by the harness. As she sways, her eyes are drawn down to see a gaping hole of a *massive* Elite that takes up half of the building's width. The inside looks like swirling mercury.

She screams, but it comes out as a muffled cry as tears stream down her cheeks. Yanking her gaze away, she searches the area frantically.

Several people are watching as she is lowered into the huge Elite. Most have blank expressions, but there are a few who have looks of pity. Movement along the far wall catches her eye as Crom slips in through a back door.

As soon as he sees her, the bag slips from his fingers. He sinks to his knees as his hand covers his mouth, a look of horror on his face. At that moment, she knows she is doomed.

She struggles against her bonds even harder. Working her jaw, the gag loosens.

"Quit struggling, Queremi," the man who had tied her to the frame calls up. "The more you relax, the better it will be. The Elite Elder has selected you personally; you should be honored."

Finally free of the sticky cloth, she sucks in a hot breath. "No! Please don't!" She screams at the auburn-haired man. "Let me go! Please!"

His face clouds over as soon as he hears her voice. "You will soon understand."

The frame lurches once before plunging into the Elite.

A shriek erupts from Emi's lips. Closing her eyes, she wonders what will happen once she hits that silvery goo beneath her. Will she splat and die instantly, or will she sink and drown?

The frame beneath her feet takes the initial impact.

Jarred, her eyes fly open and look across the milling people as Crom staggers closer, devastation written all over his face.

Her legs sink into the silvery substance. It is thick like mud but hot like simmering water. She cringes away from it to find that the cloth bonds around her feet have dissolved as well as the bottom hem of her pants.

She stares at the thin stretch of skin just visible above the surface. The silvery liquid has already turned her skin a vivid, bright pink. She looks up again, despairing as a choked sob escapes her lips.

She knows it is already too late. She can't move, and Crom is too far away to help – not that he can. She sinks deeper and deeper into the hot, viscous material. It feels like ages yet mere seconds by the time it encloses her chest.

She can't breathe. The heat and thickness of the liquid compresses around her like a contracting muscle. She struggles to keep her head above the surface; even though the bindings around her hands have dissolved, she can't stay afloat. She sucks in one last desperate breath and squeezes her eyes shut.

Something pulls her under.

She tries her hardest to swim up, but her arms barely move in the thickening material. It cools around her just enough so it isn't burning her, but this by no means helps the lack of air or her inability to move.

As the seconds slowly turn into minutes, she can't hold her breath any longer and chokes. The liquid burns as it slides down her windpipe and pools in her lungs. She reflexively tries to cough it up, but she ends up swallowing more, instead. Everything burns as she drowns in the thick, hot liquid.

Just a week ago, she had been looking at a tulip in the

woods with Crom. Now, she is in the belly of an Elite, the very beings that are supposed to be *protecting* humans, not eating them.

This is it.

She can't see. She can't hear. She can't think. She can't *breathe.*

I'm going to die.

A flicker of light dances in front of her.

She reaches out reflexively and cups the light in her hand, barely registering that her body is moving as though she is in regular water. She curls around the small orb, feeling somehow comforted by it.

As she stares at the pretty glow, it takes her a moment to realize she is still conscious.

She tries frowning, but she feels nothing.

She opens her mouth to speak, yet no sound comes out.

When she turns her head, all she sees is darkness.

Where... am I? she wonders, trying to figure out what is happening. Wasn't she just eaten by the Elite Elder?

A larger glowing orb floats in front of her. Following this one, she finds herself in a small field. Looking down, she sees tiny, dead trees and strange, miniature creatures that kneel and grovel at her feet.

She must be dreaming.

Seeing another light, she follows this one to a city. The walls are nearly as tall as her, and she reaches out to touch them. Her arm is a smooth rod that tapers to a spindly end. She stares at it in shock, but her body continues to move on its own.

She is inside an Elite.

Chapter 8

Crom sinks to his knees, unable to support himself. Emi's screams echo in his head, and he feels dizzy.

He had failed.

Bile rises into his mouth, and the acrid taste is hard to swallow. Emi is in the Elite Elder, her very life being used as sustenance for the giant creature. Now, even if she comes out, she will never be the same. Being a part of the Elite messes with people.

He drags himself onto a bench. Staring at his feet, he mulls over the plan to escape. Originally, he had wanted to leave at nighttime and head to the northwest edge of the wall; it is the closest to the warehouse, and he had found a door along the wall where they can escape. The inside of the wall is a labyrinth, so finding their way out won't be easy, but it should be doable.

Now, though, he has to wait for Emi to emerge from the Elite Elder. This is her first time, so she will only be inside the Elder for a couple of hours; however, her condition afterward will determine what they do from here on out.

Clenching his fists, he glares at the Elite. The opening in its chest slowly melds back into place as though it had never been a gaping hole. Within the span of a few minutes, it is completely sealed off with no signs of the human it had eaten.

The harness that had sentenced her to her fate swings in the air like a noose, empty and forlorn.

Emi stares blankly through the eyes of the Elite Elder. She has absolutely no control over this monster; it does what it wants. She is simply an unlucky passenger whisking from one memory fragment to the next.

In this scene, she witnesses the Elite's mothership landing on another unfortunate planet on the brink of destruction. The residents are in a terrible war with one another, nearly wiping out their own kind in the process of dominance. They are four-legged creatures with strange, flat faces and winglike contraptions on their back. They are sleek and elegant in their own way, but so fundamentally different than anything Emi has seen before that she can't help but shiver. When the Elites arrive, they stop fighting just long enough to see if they are friend or foe – which is all the time the extraterrestrial invaders need.

The Elite Elder extends its spindly arm, coming to an agreement with the denizens of the world. Emi watches dully as yet another world succumbs to the dominance of the Ravremshrua, which is what the Elites call themselves. They can't survive without a biological life force within them; they are nothing but advanced technology that outgrew the species that had created them. The one Emi is within now is one of the oldest, and it is on its last repair before it breaks down to 'birth' a new Elite. The Elites call it Emoraou, though humans know it as the Elite Elder.

A glowing orb floats in front of her face. By now, she knows these are memories of some sort, but she is already sick of following them. All scenarios turn out the same on every world the Ravremshrua visit; they find a planet on the brink of destruction, offer their support in return for the inhabitants' lives, and then leave once the world is depleted of whatever they needed. Each planet is only the span of a couple generations for the Elite, but she can see it is centuries to the denizens.

The light swirls around her, becoming more demanding. She turns to follow it, but the dull screams of the current world's citizens have her turning back to the memory.

She sees Elites hunting down the strange creatures, snatching up as many of them as possible and engulfing them within themselves. The Emoraou she is within turns and heads to their ship. It has already scooped up about fifteen denizens and gobbled them up, and Emi has the strange sensation of feeling the energy coursing through it.

It approaches the middle of the ship half-buried in the ground; the main structure it walks into looks exactly like Soltara Temple. As the Temple lifts into the air, the circular wall rises with it and exposes the underbelly of the mothership. It hovers just above the ground as the rest of the Elites clamor on, dragging the world's denizens with them.

Shivering, Emi squeezes her eyes shut. She wants it to stop. Even though she knows the Elites would most likely die on the way to the next world if they didn't do this, it isn't right to wipe out nearly a whole civilization just to keep surviving.

Everything goes quiet.

Slowly opening her eyes, she finds herself in Soltara Temple again – now, though, she knows that the Temple is merely a front entrance to the Elites' mothership. The Emoraou is slumped on the ground, unmoving as the denizens they had kidnapped shuffle around and tend to it and the other Elites.

Many of the denizens look strange now; their skin is a dark grey and looks like stone instead of fur. Their faces are permanently twisted in pain, and they now remind Emi of pictures from the old-world literature books of demonic statues and gargoyles.

The Elite Elder weakly touches one of the creatures. It falls to its knees and trembles in terror, its face twisting further into that snarling mask. All of the denizens scatter, getting out of reach of the Emoraou.

However, it does nothing. It slumps back down, and Emi can *feel* its exhaustion. They are all dying; the Elites and these creatures. The Elite Elder is waiting until the last minute to replace the denizen within itself, spending all of the poor creature's life force to keep itself alive.

Its vision goes black just as another orb of light floats by. It comes closer than ever before, and Emi closes her eyes against its light. When she opens them again, the entire ship is shaking violently. The Emoraou is at the pinnacle on a platform that controls the ship, staring out the window and through the screens at the beautiful blue and green planet below.

This planet looks like pictures of Earth.

The landing is a rather rough one, and it is in the middle of huge, towering buildings that stretch accusing fingers into the sky and rival the Elites' size. *A city*, Emi thinks dully, her first coherent thought in what feels like forever.

The city isn't like the pictures she had seen, though. Explosions have already demolished most of the buildings, reducing it to rubble-filled craters.

The Elites explore the area, not finding many people. Whoever they do find run in terror, but they are easily caught and absorbed. They allow the denizens to roam, giving them freedom. The gargoyle-like creatures quickly set up residence and claim the area, hunting down and bringing the humans to the mothership in order to set free the rest of their kind.

The humans thrive in their small villages and towns despite the state of the demolished cities that dot over half the world, so the liberated denizens have plenty of new fodder to bring back to the Elites.

The Ravremshrua take any human they can to replenish their energy. Once stronger, they free the remaining denizens from the last world that are still alive.

Once both species are back to full health, the Elites remove themselves from the city, giving the territory to the denizens for their own use. The gargoyle-like creatures roar as the ship floats away, their grating voices sounding like boulders crashing against one another.

The Elites set up their base in the middle of the forest on top of a large hill. The smaller Elites hunt the humans like deer while others remain behind and tend to their own. Many travel far and wide to explore, and even the Elite Elder traverses the blue and green planet to see the wonders of this world. It creates treaties with some humans and demolishes others who refuse to cooperate.

Emi is horrified. Unlike the other worlds, humanity had not been on the brink of destruction. The *Elites* are what wiped out the majority of the populace.

An image of a middle-aged man smiling up at the Elite Elder burns itself into her brain. *That's General Fletcher,* she realizes, recognizing him from pictures. *He's the one who created the civilization we now live in with the Elite.*

He brings forward a wide-eyed young woman who looks strangely like Emi. Her red hair shines in the sunlight like fire, and the Elite Elder is awed by the brilliant red. According to General Fletcher, she had killed her spouse.

He's the one who offered us up.

From then on, the Elites only take those who are offered to them. Most are criminals or killers like the red-haired woman. They also request that red-haired individuals work directly with them; apparently, the Elites are fascinated with the bright, vibrant color and wish to see it often.

Crime is reduced over time due to the fear of being offered up to the Elites, so a new treaty had to be created. Since the Elites do not have to kill the people they use, the general recommends to use a handful of humans to cycle through. They and their families are compensated accordingly, of course, and everyone can continue living in peace.

After a few decades, most people forget that the Elites use their kind like fodder. They grow accustomed to living alongside them, and the 'chosen' ones are kept separate from their own kind to keep them close at hand and reduce rebellion.

It is a perfect scenario for the Ravremshrua.

Chapter 9

Crom waits anxiously on the platform next to the swirling liquid that separates him from the Elite Elder's innards. He normally prefers to be in the front of the warehouse fixing the machines or inventorying the storage rooms, not pulling people out of the Elites.

This time, he is happy he will be the one who gets slimed.

Vivid red hair swirls underneath the surface of the liquid. Reaching in, he fights against the thick fluid and pulls Emi out with a hard yank. It takes quite a bit of strength and manipulation due to the Elite's strange inner fluid that acts like a contracting muscle.

He hooks his arms underneath Emi's shoulders, managing to pull her halfway out when the liquid suddenly relaxes around her. They topple onto the platform, and his head thumps painfully against the solid metal. Wincing, he focuses on the woman sprawled across him. Only a thick, silvery fluid covers her raw, pink skin.

As the platform slowly descends, Crom carefully inspects Emi as he pulls a thin blanket over her to preserve at least a bit of her modesty. The metallic fluid of the Elite coats her skin, but it hardly disguises anything.

For a brief second, he remembers the first couple of times he had pulled someone out of an Elite. He had been so embarrassed at seeing a naked person. Now, though, he thinks nothing of it as he checks for any marks or bruises on her skin. He rubs his thumb over her arms, wiping away some of the shiny fluid. He doesn't see anything.

This is a good sign. Those who come out with marks or bruises typically had some sort of mental breakdown while inside the Elite, and the injuries are self-inflicted by gripping or even clawing at themselves despite the mild paralyzation by the Elite's inner fluids.

He rubs Emi's shoulders and upper back in concern; she needs to cough up the fluid. Just as the lift comes to a shuddering halt, her body jerks against his. She heaves on the platform next to him and struggles to breath.

Shifting to prop himself on his arm, he readjusts her so she more easily dispels the fluid in her lungs. He pats her back and presses his cheek against the top of her head, ignoring the strange smell of stone and metal.

"I got you," he murmurs. "You're free now."

She takes a shuddering breath, her entire body trembling. The platform gate opens, and Crom carefully lifts her after ensuring the blanket won't fall off. He carries her to the floating tables as a red-haired woman trails next to him and wipes at Emi's mouth, eyes, and ears with a cloth.

"It looks like she fared well," Sinora says in her odd, distant voice. The caretaker gives him a strong yet vacant smile. "We may have another one."

He doesn't respond. He doesn't know which is worse: a raving mad or a brainwashed Emi.

As soon as he sets her down on the cot, they roll it away to tend to her. Just before she is out of sight, though, he catches a glimpse of her brilliant green eyes staring at him dazedly. She mouths only one word, but it is enough to send a spear of hope through his chest.

"Crom…"

Trying to pass the time, he returns to the lift to clean it, but someone else had beaten him to it. He heads to the locker room and pulls out one of his spare outfits from his locker. Stripping down, he quickly washes off with a damp rag and tosses the slimed clothes into a hamper. All the clothes are labeled and washed daily, so he knows this outfit will be clean and folded neatly in his locker the next day.

Walking back into the main chamber, his attention is drawn to the giant Elite Elder. The next energizer must have been easier to insert into the Elite than Emi because it is already stirring. Its entire body groans like weathered stone under pressure as it lumbers deeper into the warehouse. It is so big it has to crawl through the space; despite this, its head stretches up to half the room's height.

Crom has always wondered about its exact measurements. He estimates it is about six stories tall. Despite its size, it is careful to allow the humans below to get out of the way.

While most people have only heard tales of the Elite Elder, very few have had the 'honor' of seeing it themselves. Here in the warehouse, though, it is a regular.

As it lumbers into the last section of the warehouse, Crom exhales a breath he had been subconsciously holding. Motion near the entrance to the showers draws his attention back to the more human-sized area.

Emi shuffles aimlessly as two women tie a loose gown on her. Her eyes are wide as she stares at her feet. She mutters to no one in particular, but the nurses next to her are tight-jawed and exchanging glances and heated whispers with Sinora. The caretaker quickly steps into a room where they keep the medications.

Crom hurries forward, dread creeping into his step. As he gets close enough to hear Emi's hoarse words, the spear of hope he had felt earlier twists painfully.

"All of them… absorbed. Gone. Elites now. I'm next. I just know it… I'm next. I'm just the embryo. Food for the baby. I won't even know it… Poof. Just gone." Her eyes are glassy, and she still occasionally coughs up the fluid from the Elite.

Crom stops Sinora as she exits the medication storage room with a syringe in her hand. "Let me try," he requests.

Sinora nods and lowers the syringe, watching him.

As soon as Emi sees him, their eyes meet. He can see the crazed look in her eyes, and his heart sinks even further.

"Emi, it's okay," he reassures her half-heartedly, knowing it is futile at this point. She is already lost to the madness of whatever she had seen in the Elite. "You're out now. You can relax."

To his surprise, she slowly sinks to the floor as her gaze drills into him. "Crom, please stop them. I-I don't want to be – " She chokes and coughs up more of the silvery fluid.

He kneels in front of her and rests his hand on her shoulder. "Just take a deep breath," he murmurs, feeling as if he is looking through a window. Everything seems surreal. "You still have fluid in your lungs; you need to calm down so we can help you get it out before you pass out."

She sucks in one breath after another, staring at him as though he is her lifeline. After a brief moment, she coughs roughly and spits up several globs of the fluid. She then leans forward and rests her head against his shoulder. She trembles, but her ragged breathing is evening out.

Sinora pats his shoulder. "It seems as though you calm her. Could you stay with her for now?"

Crom nods mutely. He moves to stand, but Emi's fingers dig into his skin. He winces at her icy grip.

Her breathing hitches. "Don't – don't leave me," she whispers, and he barely hears her through the bustling sound of the nurses scurrying about. "Don't leave me with these monsters."

"I'm not leaving you," he reassures her, frowning. Who is she calling 'monsters'? The Elite or the caretakers? "I would like to sit down, though. Do you want to change? I have your clothes."

Sinora overhears him and thankfully mistakes the meaning behind his words. She smiles at him. "You must have known her beforehand. That was nice of you to grab her things."

He self-consciously shrugs. "I just wanted to help her transition on her first day," he covers up.

"You are a very kind friend." She walks away, leaving them alone.

Emi slowly raises her head. Her wide eyes stare into his, searching. "Help… transition?"

"Let's get you into some better clothes," Crom distracts her. "I left the bag near the lockers, so you can change there."

He helps her up. She doesn't make a sound other than the quiet shuffle of her feet as he walks her to the other side of the huge room. She keeps her eyes downcast, but her hand squeezes his, refusing to let go.

Chapter 10

Emi's lungs feel heavy. Every breath is a struggle; she coughs, staggering over her own feet. Her skin feels strange, and her pounding heart hammers in her ears, sounding foreign and unfamiliar.

Crom leads her through some doors before finally stopping. They are in a storage room full of rows of lockers and crates. He gently guides her to the seat before rummaging through one of the crates.

She inhales one wet breath after another, trying to acclimate back to her own body. Raising her hand to her chest, she feels the thin cloth covering her. She looks down to see the smooth, grey-white gown that streamlines her form and is instantly reminded of the Elite's cold, smooth skin.

Her voice comes out as a strangled yelp. She tugs at the gown frantically; she doesn't want to be that monster. She can't stand it.

Suddenly, Crom is there, tugging her hands away. "Hey, hey," he tries to sooth her. He stares into her eyes, searching. "What's wrong?"

"I – I – " The words clam up in her. A tear slips down her cheek. Does he think she is crazy? Will he even be able to understand what she is going through?

He kneels in front of her and squeezes her hands.

"I'm here. You're safe," he reassures her.

"Crom…" Emi finally manages to say. "I'm… me, right? Human?"

"Yes," he whispers, confused. "You're human."

"They're monsters." Her voice is barely a breath as the words tumble out. "They-they *use* us. Our city's founder *gave* us to them." She releases one of his hands to press her palm against her mouth. Her stomach roils, threatening to heave despite being empty. She can still taste the metallic and stony twang of the Elite.

"I know." He hangs his head in shame. "I've been trying to find a way to fight them, but there's nothing. Nothing! It kills me anytime someone goes into one. I don't know if they'll come out alive or dead or – " He tangles his fingers in his hair, expelling his frustration in a whoosh.

"Or crazy," Emi finishes in a low voice.

He looks at her guiltily. "I didn't mean – "

"No, I get it." She gives him a wobbly smile. "I thought I was going to go insane. Thank you for pulling me out." She squeezes her eyes shut tightly. "When I woke up, I didn't even fully realize I had control over my own body again. I kept tossing about, muttering, even clawing at the air… I *was* going insane." She glances worriedly at the door, wondering if someone will come in and cart her away.

He snorts. "That's actually pretty common around here, so don't worry about it." He rubs her hands again.

She nods mutely, not able to look at him anymore. He ruffles through his bag, pulling out some clothes. He has a dubious expression as he turns to her. In his hand is a dark blue shirt with flower designs and black pants. "I… didn't know what to grab, so I got what I could. I hope it's good enough."

Emi gives him a small smile. "Those are my favorite," she whispers, already reaching for them. "Thank you so much, Crom."

He turns around, giving her privacy. She is grateful

that he doesn't leave. She no longer trusts herself or her own actions. The sensation of being trapped in the Elite's mind with no control over its actions is still too fresh. She occasionally digs her fingernails into her palm to check if she is still in control.

She changes as fast as she can, but once she tries to put on the shirt, it fights her. She struggles to get it over her head, realizing belatedly that her arms aren't working right. Huffing in irritation and mild embarrassment, she drops her arms as much as she can; her wrists are stuck in the sleeves somehow, but she can't push them through or pull them out. At least her chest is covered – sort of, anyway.

"Uh, Crom," Emi starts hesitantly. "Can you help me? Something's wrong."

"They must not have told you," he murmurs, slowly turning around. He keeps his eyes focused on her face as he reaches up and pulls the shirt sleeve over her arm. "Something about the fluid in the Elite paralyzes you to keep you from kicking about inside of it. When you come out, you're still affected from the fluid you had ingested. It will wear off in the next hour or so."

She shivers violently as he pulls the shirt over her stomach. His hand lingers on her side as he watches her in concern.

"Are you all right?" he asks.

"Y-yes." She crosses her arms over her chest, shivering again. She is cold, but the shivers are more related to the idea that she had been paralyzed. She feels her stomach rumble under her hand, and she can no longer ignore the incessant gnawing sensation. "Is there any food? I think I should eat." *At least then, I'll have something to throw up,* she thinks.

"Of course." He takes his hand away from her waist,

and she immediately feels the lack of warmth. She shivers again as he walks to one of the lockers and opens it to reveal uniforms like the one he is wearing. He reaches into the shelf above and pulls out a little to-go box. "Here; I packed it this morning."

She doesn't have the energy to refuse; her hand trembles violently as she takes it from him. He steadies it, closing her fingers around the bread. It looks like there is honey on it.

"How can you stand it here?" Emi asks, her voice barely a breath. She nibbles on the crust.

"I have to." He sits on the bench across from her. "If I don't, I could end up in one of those Elites and just not come out. They like to keep this all a secret from everyone else."

"You said you have a plan, though," Emi whispers, staring at the floor now.

"I do." He pauses, staring intently at her. "It's not a guarantee, though. If we fail, we'll both be dead."

She knows that; she had seen it through the Elite's eyes. She had felt it grow stronger as it sucked every last drop of life out of the poor creatures that tried to flee. She doesn't want to experience the other end of that, but if her options are between dying quickly or being fodder for the rest of her life, she would rather take the faster death.

"We should try," she whispers, gazing back into his eyes. She can see the surprise there; he must have thought for a while that she had lost her mind. "You said you didn't know their weakness, right? I can help with that."

Chapter 11

Crom stares at her, not sure if he actually wants to know or not. What if it is something impossible for them to acquire? What if it isn't even a true weakness that stops them, but just momentarily slows them down?

Emi sees the look on his face and smiles. It is a tired, shaky smile, but he can see the determination and strength coming back. She had been on the border of losing her mind and becoming a listless puppet like so many others, but he can tell she is slowly piecing her composure back together.

"It's the mirrors," she whispers. "More than that, though, it's what most mirrors are *made* out of. Silver."

Silver.

A rare metal that is said to have been a prominent part of society before the Devastation. It is rumored to be a pure, shiny grey-white, and the name for the color silver had originated from the very metal. Not many have had the honor of seeing this metal, and if they did, they raved at how pretty it is and how it never rusts.

"We don't have silver, though," Crom barely breathes. He feels as though the world is going to crash in around him; the sliver of hope inside him twists painfully in his chest.

"Yes, we do." Emi's smile strengthens into a triumphant grin. "In my house."

He stares at her for a long moment before realization hits him. "You... you can't mean..."

"Yes." She clenches her fists. "We break my mirror,

and we use it against them."

The spark of hope lights inside him again. "What does it do to them?" he asks, already standing up and throwing the bag over his shoulder.

Emi gets to her feet, a little wobbly. "It poisons them," she explains shakily, a small frown marring her face. "I don't know why, but… it's like a chemical reaction. Their bodies can't handle silver, and they crack. The more they are exposed to, the more they crack until they start falling apart."

"Huh." He shuts the locker door and turns to her, a deep frown on his face. "Will your mirror be enough, then?"

"I don't know." Her voice is barely over a breath. "It doesn't take much, though. I remember seeing through the Emoraou that a younger Elite had merely touched a silver plate, and its entire arm had crumbled and fell off. That's why anything made of silver is not allowed around the Elites."

Emoraou. A shiver crawls up Crom's spine; not many know that word, and even he isn't completely sure what it means. Only those who have been energized for extended periods of time start saying that word.

"Emi…" He watches her awkward movements as she folds the gown the nurses had put her in. There is something eerily familiar about it. He doesn't want to think too hard on it, but he needs to make sure. "Are you sure you're up to doing this?"

She glances at him, and he sees a hint of crazed fear still lurking in the young woman. "I think so." She struggles to find the words. "Being inside the Emoraou did something to me. I can tell. I-I don't know exactly what yet, but…"

There it is again. "Emoraou," he repeats slowly. Now

is his chance to confirm his suspicions on that word. "Is that the Elite Elder?"

"Yes." Her voice is barely a breath. "It's… it's the closest I can pronounce its actual name. The Elites have their own language, but they learn to replicate other sounds. 'Elite' is just what they gave us to call them so we had a name. It's actually something like Ravremshrua."

Crom takes a deep breath, not even trying to pronounce that one. He turns and walks down the row of lockers. He pauses, though, as a thought crosses his mind. Turning around, he stops Emi as she tries to follow him.

"Emi, you can't come with me," he tells her as gently as he can. "If you left the building, it would raise an alarm, and everyone would be on alert for the next several days. I'll be back as soon as possible, though."

She crosses her arms, hugging herself tightly. "But…"

"They won't put you back in tonight," he reassures her. "They always let you rest before another energizing session. Do you remember where I showed you the flower?"

She nods.

"If I'm not back by nightfall, go there. There's a side entrance at the back of this room; you don't need a key card to leave." He pauses, watching her for a moment longer. "Make sure to take the cuff off so you aren't followed. We're given a bit of leeway once it's late evening, but even then, we need to be careful not to be spotted once we leave the warehouse."

She nods again. She still has a lost look on her face. "Crom…" she finally says, her voice shaky. "Please… please be careful. The Emoraou – the Elder – it's taken an interest in you because you pulled me out. I-I can just tell."

A chill slides down his spine. He turns so he is fully

facing her, and his eyes narrow. "How do you know?"

She touches her temple, her face going white again. She slumps back onto the bench. "It's still in my head," she whispers. "I can… I can feel it. It's hunger and stiffness and coldness. It's so old, Crom, but it's also not so weak it can't stop us."

"Do you think it can sense things on your side, too?" he asks, suddenly worried.

She shakes her head. "I-I don't think so."

He swallows the uneasy feeling in the pit of his stomach. This new knowledge about the Elites and now the Elite Elder is a double-edged sword. On one hand, it helps them plan their escape; however, if Emi has become their spy and is tricking him, he will be playing right into their trap.

As he slips out of the locker room, he hears the brainwashed caretakers calling out and talking to Emi. He struggles not to think of how easily everything can end right then and there if she decides to expose their plan.

Once he is in town, he sneaks through deserted alleys and back roads the best he can. Being in cleaner clothes definitely helps him blend in, but people can still recognize the garb of those who work at the warehouse and know he shouldn't be in the city during the night. His place of rest is the warehouse; there are living quarters for the workers inside. His very presence in town is suspicious.

Crom finally makes it to Emi's house a little after sunset. Slipping in through the back door, he once again wonders why she doesn't lock it. Going to her room, he stares at the floor-length mirror intently, still in disbelief that this relic of their old world is what he has been looking for all along.

He slowly walks up to it, trying hard not to stare at his grungy appearance. Despite the cleaner clothes, there are oil-like stains in the material that won't come out no matter what, making him look permanently dirty.

Reaching out, he brushes his hand along the edge of the mirror, feeling the curving rivulets and dips in the metal. Curling his fingers around the solid frame, he mentally apologizes to Emi's family for what he is about to do.

He yanks it toward himself, tipping it over. Its momentum and weight carry it to the hard floor as he steps out of the way.

It crashes, splintering and tinkling. He flinches at the harsh sound.

It is much, *much* louder than he had anticipated.

Chapter 12

Glancing at the door, Crom quickly kneels down and picks up the largest piece. He had made the stupidest mistake possible in this district: caused a commotion. Now, concerned neighbors might come over and see what is wrong. He needs to hurry and –

"Ow!" he yelps, surprised at the sharp pain in his thumb. He stares in rapt fascination as a droplet of blood wells and then falls on the shattered mirror fragment, staining the piece he had been trying to pick up. The cut is deep; he finds it hard to believe such a wound was inflicted by the shattered pieces.

Sticking the tip of his thumb in his mouth and tasting the coppery fluid, he gingerly picks up a few pieces. He is careful to not slice himself open again as he gently puts them in his bag. He pulls a shirt from Emi's drawer to cushion them so they don't clink or – even worse – cut a hole in the bag.

Creeeaaak.

"Emi? Is everything okay? I heard a loud crash," a feminine voice calls from the front of the house.

Crom whirls around, his eyes wide. If someone from the warehouse catches him here now, it will be over. If it's a neighbor, he might be able to talk himself out of trouble.

He picks up a heavy-looking metal box on Emi's dresser. An antique by the looks of it. He doesn't want to use it against someone who is likely Emi's friend, but he will do what he needs to in order to keep their plan a secret.

Their lives depend on it.

"Emi? Are you here?"

He clenches his hand around the box, the pain of the mirror shard slicing into it forgotten.

"That's right. Emi got the Witch's Doll," the feminine voice comments to herself, and he hears her stop halfway down the hall. "She won't be here… But then what made that sound?"

She talks out loud too much, Crom grumbles to himself, narrowing his eyes at the doorway. He slips behind the door just as the woman peeks into the room.

"Hello?" she asks the room cautiously. "If anyone's in here, you're not supposed to be here. Please come out…"

She sucks in her breath, and Crom intuitively knows she is staring at the broken mirror. "Oh, no, no, no… She's going to be so upset!" The woman mutters to herself, rushing forward and kneeling next to the shattered pieces of the mirror. She looks to be about the same age as Emi and Crom, but he can tell by how she talks that she mustn't be too bright. She is dressed similarly to how Emi had been dressed a week ago, and he guesses she is also a librarian.

As she stacks the pieces together, he uses this opportunity to sneak around the door and into the hallway. He can probably get out without being discovered.

"How can I put this back together without her noticing… Hmm?"

Glancing back, he catches sight of her examining the mirror shard with red blood smeared on it.

Shit. He moves as quietly as he can. *I need to get out of here* now.

He creeps down the hallway, trying to not make a

sound. Keeping a hold of the jewelry box just in case he needs to use it, Crom slips into the living room and makes his way to the back door. If he can avoid Emi's friend, it will make his job here easier.

"Stop right there!"

Crom slowly turns around to face the quivering voice. The young woman stands at the entrance to the hallway, and she holds a shard of glass upright with both hands. He can see a small trickle of blood trailing down her palms from where she grips the shard.

He slowly holds up his hands. "Hey there," he greets in a calm voice, trying to not aggravate her. "I didn't mean to startle you. I just dropped by to pick up some stuff for Emi; I didn't even realize someone else was here."

Her hand wavers. "When did you get here?"

"Just now," he lies; librarians don't know the normal procedure for Emi's type of Calling, so he should be able to bluff his way through it. "She wanted me to pick up some things, but I don't really know where everything is."

She lowers the glass shard even more and nods behind herself. "Her room is back here. Do you need any help finding anything?"

"I should be fine." He examines her hand in feigned curiosity. "What happened? What is that thing?"

She looks at her bloodied hands, a little embarrassed. "It's a piece of her mirror," she admits, letting go of her death grip and flexing her hands with a wince. The shard clatters to the ground with a tinkling sound. "I thought I heard someone come in earlier, but when I went back to her room, all I saw was her broken mirror."

His eyebrows snap together in feigned concern. "Her mirror broke? That's not good," he reiterates, feigning ignorance. "I know it was special to her. Are you all right?"

"Yeah, I think so. It just scratched me." She glances

at his bag. "I can help you find what you need."

He quickly shakes his head. "You should get that checked out. It looks serious."

She is already walking down the hallway. She turns right into a different room, and he cautiously follows to discover it is a bathroom. "Emi keeps some stuff in her cabinet because she's so prone to injuries," the young woman says wryly, throwing him a smile over her shoulder. "I should be able to find something in here."

She opens a cabinet to reveal a sterilizing strip, bandages, and gauze. As she dresses her wounds, she introduces herself, "I'm Sophie, by the way. I live next door. And you are?"

"Cory," he lies again as he slips the jewelry box surreptitiously into his bag.

"Good to meet you, Cory," she hums as she puts up the supplies and closes the cabinet. "So what does she need?"

"Clothes," he admits. It is quite common knowledge that people wear their own clothes around the warehouse unless they are part of the maintenance or extraction crew. It gives him an excuse to be there, after all.

"Oh, I can help with that! I know what she likes." She walks toward Emi's room before he can stop her.

"Thank you," he says, worried it might seem suspicious if he refuses her help. "I wouldn't even know where to begin."

"It's no problem. Her clothes are in here. She likes the ones with patterns on them the most. I'll grab the undergarments." She gives him a knowing look before rummaging through the drawers.

Crom is secretly grateful that Sophie is taking care of that. Flipping through the clothes, he takes a few long-sleeved shirts off their hangers and folds them neatly. At least this is giving him an excuse to grab more clothes for Emi as well as pad the mirror fragments a bit better. Before he can shove them in the bag, though, Sophie glances over.

"Why are you grabbing the long-sleeved shirts?" she asks in curiosity. "Won't she be warm?"

He shrugs. "Doesn't seem that way. I was requested to bring some back."

"Oh."

As he pulls down a jacket, she stands up. He glances at her, a little taken aback by her frown. "What is it?"

"The clothes you're grabbing…" She stares at him hard. "They're outdoor clothes. She shouldn't need those."

He glances down at the small pile in his arms. Laughing awkwardly, he reaches for a cute tank top as he mentally berates himself. "I guess you're right," he agrees as he folds the shirt and grabs another. "I'm really not used to grabbing this sort of stuff."

"I can always take it to her," Sophie offers, putting some undergarments in a small bag she finds under the bed.

Crom shakes his head. "Nah, I got it. Anyway, you're not allowed in the warehouse."

"You must be new." She finishes up and throws the bag over her shoulder. She turns to see his startled look and gives him a knowing smile. "Normally, I'm in the library helping the Elites as one of the head librarians; Emi used to work under me. Now and then, though, they ask for my help in the warehouse."

Chapter 13

Crom's blood chills. He has heard that some individuals who are strangely loyal are integrated back into society after they work for the Elites for a certain amount of time, but he never thought one would look so young. "You… but how?"

She pats her hair, fluffing it a little. "I look good for my age, don't I?" She teases at the confusion on his face. "I was with the Elites for about ten years before they rewarded my loyalty and transferred me to the library to work with the Emoraou." She gives him a piercing glare. "Now, though, I would like to know why someone like *you* was sent to retrieve Emi's things and not myself or Sinora."

He can't move. He stares at her, unable to believe that she is one of the few who have been integrated back into society. He scrambles to find words to defend himself.

"I don't know what you're talking about," he finally manages to get out, but it sounds like a lame excuse even to him.

"Oh, don't play with me. You know that others more suitable are tasked with this sort of thing." She walks toward him. "What were you planning on doing?"

He hardens his resolve, not allowing himself to be intimidated by this person who is no longer human. She is as bad as the Elite. "Everybody was focused on taking care of the energizers," he tries explaining. "Since I know Emi, I wanted to help her."

Sophie crosses her arms, a dubious look on her face.

"So those warmer clothes aren't for anything... special?"

"What would I use them for?" he asks, trying to play ignorant.

She narrows her eyes, watching him in suspicion. After a moment, her expression softens into a frown. She waves her hand dismissively. "Let us return to the warehouse," she says, walking to the door. "I would like to check on the progress of Emi, anyway. She was a good friend and coworker of mine."

As soon as she steps past Crom, he quickly pulls out the box from his bag and hits the nape of her neck. She falls just like the mirror had but lands with a dull thud instead of a resounding crash.

"Not sorry," he says without a shred of remorse, shifting his bag on his shoulder into a more comfortable position as he steps over her limp body and walks out the door. He quietly shuts it behind himself, hurrying along the alleys and side paths.

By the time he makes it back to the warehouse, he is sweating with anticipation. He hopes and prays to some higher being that Sophie has not woken up yet. Glancing at the stars above, he hurries around to the back of the warehouse where the tulip should still be.

A figure hunches over the fragile flower, examining it intensely. As he cautiously draws closer, it turns around to reveal Emi staring at him with wide eyes and a terrified expression.

"It's just me," Crom quickly says, holding up his hands. "Were you followed?"

She shakes her head. "I don't think so." She eyes him closely. "Did you get it?"

He nods. Reaching into the bag, he gingerly pulls out one of the mirror fragments from the bottom. As he turns it toward her, it reflects the moonlight from above, flashing across her face.

She reaches out and takes the shard. Turning it carefully in her hands, she breathes, "Let's hope this works."

Before he can respond, a harsh, high-pitched whistling sound comes from the other side of the warehouse. Crom twists around, his heart hammering in his chest as his mind flashes to Sophie lying unconscious on Emi's floor.

She must have woken up and alerted the warehouse, he thinks. "Run."

Emi doesn't move. She stares over his shoulder, her eyes wide in fear.

He grabs her arm and tugs her upright. "We need to run!" he hisses in her ear, yanking her along.

She staggers after him, constantly glancing behind them with wide eyes as if expecting an Elite to crash through the woods at any moment.

They run as far and as fast as they can. They hear voices calling for them, trying to lure them back with empty promises that they won't be hurt. Crom berates himself inwardly as he realizes that his choice to spare Sophie's life is probably what revealed their plan so early.

"Crom."

He keeps running, ignoring Emi's strained breathing.

"Crom, please stop!"

She yanks his hand hard, pulling him to a stop. He whirls on her, confused and angry at her actions; she seems stronger than he had originally thought. "Emi, why did you – "

She gasps for breath. "I'm sorry," she breathes, barely getting out the words. "I can't… keep up."

He glances around, but he doesn't see anyone. "Catch your breath," he tells her in a low voice. "You're going to have to deal with it until we get past the wall."

"Okay."

He glances at her, hearing her wheezing gasps. They still sound slightly wet and forced, concerning him.

"Just hang in there," he murmurs as his hand slides down her arm to grab her wrist. They have to make it to the wall, and then they will be free.

They start running again. The minutes pass by, and he can see a smooth, dark grey structure in front of them.

Emi's breath hitches at the sight of the wall, recognizing it from the Emoraou's memories. She trips over a rock.

Crom staggers, trying not to fall with her. Looking back, he scans the trees. Nothing moves.

"Get up, Emi!" he barks, tugging on her hand.

She winces as she puts weight on her ankle. Glancing ahead, she freezes, her eyes wide. Crom follows her gaze.

A large form lumbers through the trees, walking toward them. It is one of the Elites that guard the wall, though it is on the small side; it only rises to about eight or nine feet tall.

"No," Emi breathes, staggering back. "They caught up."

Crom digs in his bag and pulls out a mirror shard. He brandishes it like a knife, holding it carefully so it doesn't slice his hand open. "Emi, start walking to the right."

Light glimmers off the silvery fragment. The Elite pauses, and Crom has the odd feeling that he is being stared at, though he can't tell for certain. Elites don't have eyes, after all. He waves the shard about as they move to the right.

The Elite doesn't move.

Emi clenches his shirt, unable to tear her eyes away from the Elite. "Crom," she breathes. "Something's not right."

"You think?!" he exclaims quietly, also not risking looking away. "We're almost there, though. Just a little farther."

As they creep in a wide circle around the Elite, it turns as if watching them. Finally, when they are nearly on the side of the wall, they start backing up.

Emi looks behind them, glimpsing the wall between the trees. She bites her lower lip, wondering if they can really make it and be free.

"I don't think it will attack us," Crom says in a low voice. "If we can just make it to – "

The Elite lunges.

Chapter 14

Crom and Emi stagger back, narrowly missing the sweeping arm of the Elite as it dives for them. Crom holds out his hand defensively, scratching its arm with the glass shard as it whizzes by. It leaves the barest of marks.

It rears back, staring at the shallow scratch on its spindly arm.

Crom yanks Emi to her feet. They slowly back up, holding their breath and hoping it works. After all, even though it is a tiny scratch, it is still silver.

A musical rumble emerges from the Elite. It twists its head toward them, the sound turning darker like a roiling thundercloud.

Emi's breath sucks in. "It didn't work," she breathes, tears pooling in her eyes. "It… it's not poisoned."

"What?!" He glares at the glass shard in his hand. Blood oozes where he clenches it tightly. "Maybe I just didn't cut it enough."

"Just *touching* silver should do it!"

He yanks on her hand, and they sprint for safety.

The Elite's rumbling ends in a giant boom that sounds like a thunderclap after lightning strikes. It lunges toward them again, both of its arms splitting apart into stony tendrils and reaching for them.

No, not both of them… just Emi.

Crom shoves her behind him, and she falls again as he raises the mirror shard up despite the painful twinge it causes. He swipes hard at the tendrils that are about to hit them, slicing deeper this time. A silvery liquid pours out, but it hardens almost instantly. Cracks crawl up the arm from the injury, and flakes of stone fall off.

The Elite yowls, withdrawing quickly. It examines the hardened wound before taking its other spindly arm, forming a blade with it, and chopping off the petrifying limb.

Crom's eyes widen. It really was because he didn't cut deeply enough. Not wanting to lose this chance, he grabs Emi by the arm and pulls her to her feet again. They run as fast as they can toward the towering wall.

"How… will we… climb it?" she gasps, her face twisted in pain as she tries to run as fast as she can on her sprained ankle.

"There's a service door," he huffs out, glancing back. The Elite is following them again, but the thicker trees hamper its movements. It has to chop them down or squeeze past them. He grins; they have a chance.

"U-up!" Emi squeaks in terror.

Crom looks up. All he can see is the wall and the sky beyond it, but he quickly spots what has her panicking.

A strange creature crouches on the edge of the wall, glaring down at them. Its eyes glow red; it looks like those pictures of the winged creatures on the sides of buildings from hundreds of years ago before the great Devastation. It screeches, an awful sound like metal scraping against glass.

"A gargoyle?!" he breathes in disbelief. It is supposed to be a statue, not an actual living thing.

"They're… still alive?" Emi breathes in shock, recognizing it from the Elite Elder's memories.

It spreads its two great wings and dives into the trees. The two humans cover their faces as twigs and pine needles swirl about them, and they brace for its claws to rip into them.

Crom feels the hair on his head stand on end as the gargoyle passes over them, making a beeline for the Elite in the trees. It barrels into the giant, biting and clawing at it viciously.

The Elite wails, its silver blood spraying all over the gargoyle. It stabs the creature with its multitude of spindly nodes, and the gargoyle screeches again as dark, murky liquid oozes from it.

The two humans slowly back up to the wall, both of them too stunned at the sudden attack to say or do anything. Emi's tight grip on Crom's arm brings him back to his senses, though, and he quickly looks along the sides of the wall for the door. Seeing it a bit farther down, he tugs her with him, heading for it.

Emi watches the fight. "It… killed the Elite," she gasps, struggling to keep up with him. "Those are the Elite's previous victims. Maybe – "

"I doubt that thing is on our side, Emi!" he barks at her.

The gargoyle screeches again, turning those blood-colored eyes their way. It growls, the sound of grating rocks coming from its maw. Leaping off the still form of the Elite, it weaves through the trees with the ease and dexterity of a creature who hunts in the forest.

Emi's shrill shriek has Crom running even faster. He rams into the door, and the weight of Emi subsequently slamming into him is enough to force it open. They tumble into the maze that is the inside the wall, sprawling across the cool floor inside. Soft light emanates from the edges of the ceiling and wall, lighting their surroundings.

Scrambling back to his feet, Crom quickly races to the door and slams it shut, blocking out the view of the gargoyle gaining on them with terrifying speed. Glancing around, he notices a crank to the side of the stone door and quickly spins it counterclockwise. A giant stone plank lowers to block the door at the same moment the gargoyle slams into it on the other side.

The entire wall shakes violently.

Backing away from it, he stares as the wall shakes again. Tiny cracks form in the stone. "Get up, Emi!"

They dash through entryways and down hallways, not knowing where to go or which way to turn to escape the mysterious wall. The screeching roar of the gargoyle follows them as their ragged breaths echo back.

Several times, they fear the gargoyle-like creature will catch up to them and eat them whole, but it is Emi at the last second who pulls Crom into another room, slams the door shut, and keeps running despite their burning lungs.

Finally, they see a glimmer of light ahead of them.

"Almost there!" Crom shouts.

They burst free, barely coming to a stop in time to keep from plummeting over a cliff. They stare out, both of them speechless as they see the world stretched in front of them for the first time in their lives.

A thick, twisted forest stretches out in front of them, and beyond that, the land rises and falls in hills that gradually become mountains. Light rising above the edge of the world illuminates the treetops. They stand on a cliff overlooking it all, and a narrow pathway leads down the side of the cliff toward the forest.

"Crom…" Emi whispers, her voice shaking as she looks down.

He doesn't say anything back.

Normally, this would have been a beautiful view. However, in the dawning light of the new day, they can see gargoyles prowling in a clearing directly below them.

Chapter 15

Gargoyles swarm around the body of an Elite that had most likely been guarding the wall. They tear at its monolithic body as it struggles weakly.

All of the gargoyles are covered in wounds, but the Elite is on death's door. Within a few more seconds, the gargoyles dispatch the huge Elite and turn their eyes upward.

Emi squeaks in terror, falling to the ground. Crom swallows hard, now realizing that there is some truth to the Elites' promise to protect them.

The world might not be a wasteland, but it is certainly dangerous past the wall. No human can survive on their own with monsters like these roaming about. In return for the Elites' protection, the humans struck a deal with them so they at least have some chance to survive.

"Heh." Crom's legs give out from under him. He can hear the growling of the gargoyle that had been chasing them; its eyes glimmer in the darkness of the corridor. "I guess this is it."

Emi shakes her head vehemently, tears streaming down her face. "No. No! It can't be!" She stands between the gargoyle and Crom. She is terrified, but her stance stays firm.

"Emi, it's okay," Crom murmurs, already resigning himself to his fate. "At least it won't be a slow one like what the Elites would do to us."

"I-I won't – " She chokes on her words, her fists

clenched tightly. "I won't give up. These creatures used to be victims, too. They're just… just angry. They're angry at the Elite for taking them away from their home and doing this to them, for mutating them. If only I could…"

Standing up, Crom wraps his arms around Emi from behind. He buries his face in her silky auburn hair, taking a deep, steadying breath. "Unless you can pull off moves like them or the Elites, we won't survive," he tells her simply as her tears hit his arm.

She hugs his arms, leaning into him for a brief moment before pushing him away, and he falls to the ground. She stares at the gargoyle defiantly. "No. I won't give up."

"Emi – "

The gargoyle springs forward, leaping out of the tunnel with incredible speed. Emi's face pales as she stares at the gargoyle bearing down on her.

What am I doing? I'm not an Elite. Even if they were converting me, I wouldn't be able to do anything, she screams at herself in her mind, leaping to the side and narrowly missing the gargoyle's sharp claws.

She sprawls across the dirt, wincing as her shoulder and arm slam into the hard ground. The gargoyle flies past, coming within mere inches of her face. It scrambles at the edge of the cliff, but its momentum sends it over. Its howl grates the air, making it feel as though reality itself will split apart.

Emi closes her eyes briefly. Her arm aches dully from the pain of landing on it. "I-I thought I was going to die."

Crom glances at the pathway leading down the cliff. He pales and tugs on Emi's good arm. "Think you can run? Or we really might."

Emi follows his gaze and chokes back a scream. The

gargoyles are creeping up the pathway, their bloodshot eyes locked on the two humans at the top. Something in their stance screams that they aren't merely hunting; they are out for blood, for vengeance. The one leading the pack straightens a little after getting a good look at them. Its eyes narrow into slits.

Emi scrambles to her feet, tugging Crom back into the tunnel as she cradles her arm. He stares at her back as they sprint through the twisting maze. "Emi, why are we – "

"Anywhere but there." Her breaths are short and ragged, and he can tell she is in a lot of pain, but she keeps running through the halls, going deeper and deeper into the maze.

They sprint through the corridors, gaining distance between themselves and the gargoyles stalking them. Suddenly, Emi pulls Crom into a room, and they push the door closed. They slump against the far wall and sink to the floor, gasping for air.

"This place. It's a refuge," Emi forces out, pulling her knees to her chest as she catches her breath.

"A… refuge?" Crom repeats, confused.

She nods. "This wall is a part of the Elites' ship, but it's where the creatures they keep usually live. It's too small for the Elite, but large enough for humans and other things our size."

He glances around. The soft light emanating from the ceiling illuminates the living quarters. There is a counter in the corner and broken furniture in the middle.

"They must have decided to build our city on top of their ship, then, but that means we haven't truly escaped." He looks at her, concern written all over his face. "Why did you do that back there?"

She closes her eyes, knowing she had almost gotten

both of them killed. "I… I thought I could fight it."

Crom pales. "What the heck made you think that?"

She gives him a tight smile. "I… guess I got carried away. Maybe I *am* going a little crazy."

Crom's head thumps against the wall weakly. His dazed eyes stare at the dim ceiling. "Sophie works for the Elite," he admits quietly, his heart twisting. "She betrayed you."

"I figured. I saw her in the Emoraou's memories." Glancing at the door, her eyes widen. She holds up a hand to silence Crom. They hold their breath as a faint sound grows louder.

Tap, tap, tap, tap.

Chapter 16

The soft clicking of nails on stone echoes down the hall outside. It stops on the other side of the door.

They hold their breath, willing their hearts to stop pounding so loudly.

The gargoyle raps at the door. Once, twice, thrice.

They don't move.

Three more raps. A growl and clicking sound comes from behind the door. The door knob slowly turns.

Blood-red eyes stare at them through the crack.

"Crap. Emi, run!" Crom snaps, scrambling to get between her and the gargoyle. This time, *he* will protect *her*.

The gargoyle growls and snaps, its face contorting in that awful, terrifying mask. It makes a series of weird clicks and whistles mixed with grunts, slowly creeping into the room.

"I-I didn't mean to!" Emi cries, anguish written all over her face. Tears spring to her eyes as she stares at the gargoyle. "Please understand. We were going to die!"

Crom glances at her, startled by her outburst. Can she understand this creature?

The gargoyle tilts its head to the side as if trying to understand. It examines her intently for a moment before making those sounds again, though they are mostly whistles now.

Emi's expression relaxes into one of shock and relief. "Really…? That's why?" She swallows hard, touching her neck as if realizing something. She clears her throat and whistles back, occasionally throwing in a click from her tongue. It is a strange combination of sounds.

Crom involuntarily steps away from her. "Emi…?" he breathes, now afraid of the red-haired woman.

Emi looks up at him from her kneeling position on the ground. Her tear-streaked face breaks into a smile as triumph shines in her eyes. "They will help us, Crom. They had attacked because they thought I was an Elite; they didn't realize we're human until they got a good look at us in the light earlier."

"So… you can understand it? And it understands you?"

She shakes her head. "It doesn't understand English, so I – " She touches her head lightly, realizing Crom's sudden wariness. Tears fill her eyes again. "I… really am becoming like them…"

The gargoyle makes those strange clicking and whistling sounds. Crom glances at it, still wary. "What's it saying?"

"It says I smell like the Elites. It's probably from when they tried to transform me." Her gaze goes glassy as she stares at her aching arm. "That's… how the Elites make more of themselves. They transform some of their victims into more of them."

"Why aren't these gargoyles like them, then?" Crom asks, gesturing to the gargoyle. It glances at him before focusing on Emi again.

"They didn't finish the process with these creatures," she explains, shivering violently. "It takes multiple sessions before an Elite is actually born. It implants memories of their kind into them, too, so that the new Elite knows what it is. That's-that's why…" She touches her head again.

That's why she knows so much. That's why she can understand the gargoyles. That's why she had thought she could fight them.

They had tried turning her into an Elite.

Crom collapses on the ground next to her. He cannot tear his gaze away from her eyes that are the same color as the trees in the forest beyond the wall that the Elite guard so zealously. His vision blurs as he touches her cheek with his fingers. "I… was too late, then?"

She shakes her head. "I don't think so. I'm still me, remember? You said so yourself."

"But… you just said…"

"If we stay, I'll really become one of them. But if we leave right now, Crom, we can *live*."

"With them?" Crom's eyes shift to the gargoyle and then back to Emi. "Are you sure they won't try to kill you again?"

"They won't. They thought I was one of the new Elites; they're really weak and easy to wipe out. That's why they attacked us on the other side of the wall. Now that they know we're human, they want to help us." Emi takes his hands. She gives him a shaky smile, trying to be strong. "Please, Crom."

His fingers clench around hers reflexively. He takes a deep breath. "Then let's get out of here."

They follow the gargoyle out of the maze, leaving behind their fate and walking into chance.

Acknowledgements

I want to thank my patrons on Patreon for all of their continual support in my publishing endeavors! A special thank you to the patrons who provided feedback and encouragement during the writing process of this story, as well.

Also, a special thank you to the following people:
– My parents, Sandie and Michael
– Barbara Dean
– Christine Stayrook
– Charles Martin
– Dedra Irwin
– Meg Lynch
– Orion Motsco
– Nathan Wind

Your continual support in my writing and my dreams fuels me! I am looking forward to providing even more amazing stories.

Craving More?

This story had originally been a Patreon exclusive for a year. Check out Maxina's Patreon for more novelettes, short stories, deleted scenes, and more!

www.patreon.com/storibrook

About the Author

Maxina Storibrook grew up traveling all over the world. She loved it so much she couldn't be satisfied by merely traveling to all the unknown places across Earth; she has to discover new places, write about other worlds, and meet amazing, adventurous people.

Maxina has a bachelor's degree in English and a master's degree in creative writing – all for the love of words. The *Danarko Saga* is her first series, and she takes pride in all the effort she has put into her realms.

In Silver Grove Publications, she hopes to bring together a family of like-minded people to bring more content to people's lives.

Her biggest dream? *To tell stories.*

————◆————

Purchase signed books, audiobooks, and ebooks on her website:
www.maxinastoribrook.com

Find out more about Silver Grove Publications and explore other SGP Authors:
www.silvergrovepublications.com